THIS BOOK BELONGS TO

For Jayden and Mr Woods ~ A.K.

For Kate, Zac, Zeb and Ziah ~ C.L.S.

INSPECTOR BRUNSWICK

The Case of the Missing Eyebrow

Angela Keoghan

Chris Lam Sam

Tate Publishing

After a long week of solving cases, Inspector Brunswick, the world's greatest cat detective, and his loyal assistant Nelson were taking a well-deserved break at the art museum.

Once inside, Brunswick was greeted by a crowd of worried faces. His whiskers began to tingle with curiosity.

"What's wrong?" he asked the puzzled museum director.

"There's something different about the portrait of The Admiral today," said the director. "But nobody knows what it is!"

Brunswick looked at the
portrait for a moment.
"Aha!" he shouted.
"I've got it..."

"...he is missing an eyebrow."

Gasps of horror went through the crowd. The director shrieked and fainted and The Admiral cried, "How embarrassing! Somebody please help me!"

"Never fear," called Nelson. "Inspector Brunswick is very good at solving mysteries, especially hairy ones."

"Yes, of course," said Brunswick "and I know exactly where the missing eyebrow is."

"Clearly," said Brunswick, "the eyebrow has floated
down from the painting and landed on someone's hat."

"Case closed!" said Nelson.

Brunswick and Nelson
searched high and low for
the missing eyebrow...

...but it was nowhere to be found.

"It's worse than I feared," said Brunswick. "This was no accident. The eyebrow has been stolen!"

The director shrieked and fainted again.

Brunswick quickly hatched a plan. He would wear a clever disguise to help him catch the eyebrow thief red-handed.

Nelson, however, had a different idea...

"Perhaps we should take a closer look at the painting, Inspector?"

"What? Oh yes, of course," said Brunswick and he whipped out his magnifying glass.

At that moment, Brunswick saw tiny footprints leading off the painting and down the wall.

"By Jove! A clue! We must follow these footprints at once."

Over...   around...
    under...   and through...

Brunswick

followed

the footprints.

The trail led them to a very odd-looking painting.
"Inspector!" cried Nelson. "You've found the missing eyebrow!"
"Oh... have I? So I have!" said Brunswick.

Brunswick plucked the
eyebrow from the painting.

"Ouch!" squeaked the eyebrow.
"Be careful with me!"

"Goodness!
I never knew eyebrows
could talk!" said Nelson.

"I'm not an eyebrow,"
said the eyebrow.
"I'm a caterpillar!"

"So it was you who stole The Admiral's eyebrow!" said Brunswick.

"I didn't steal it!" said the caterpillar. "I only painted over it and pretended to be his eyebrow for a day."

"But why would you do that?" asked Nelson.

"I'm an artist!" said the caterpillar. "People always overlook my tiny paintings. I just thought being part of some bigger paintings would help me be noticed. I am sorry for all the trouble."

Just then, Brunswick had an idea that made his whiskers tingle…

"Mr Caterpillar," said Brunswick. "I am sure I can arrange a lot more attention for a talented artist like you."

"Oh, thank you!" said the caterpillar.

That evening, Brunswick and Nelson spread the news
that the museum had agreed to exhibit new paintings by
The World's Smallest Artist, featuring the portrait of
The Admiral and his new eyebrow.

The next day, the whole town came to see the show.

Gasps of amazement came from the crowd each time the caterpillar changed The Admiral's expression. Others marvelled at the caterpillar's paintings and the director shrieked with delight.

"Case closed?" asked Nelson.

"Case closed," agreed Brunswick.

This is not an eyebrow

First published 2017 by order of the Tate Trustees
by Tate Publishing, a division of Tate Enterprises Ltd,
Millbank, London SW1P 4RG
www.tate.org.uk/publishing

A catalogue record for this book is
available from the British Library
ISBN 978-1-84976-444-5

Distributed in the United States and
Canada by ABRAMS, New York

Library of Congress Control Number applied for

Colour reproduction by
Evergreen Colour Management Ltd, Hong Kong
Printed and bound in China by Toppan Leefung Printing Ltd

MIX
Paper from
responsible sources
FSC
www.fsc.org   FSC® C104723